WHEN I WAS A LITTLE GIRL

DIYA FAROOQ AND FAKHAR INJELLA

Copyright © Diya Farooq And Fakhar Injella
All Rights Reserved.

This book has been published with all efforts taken to make the material error-free after the consent of the author. However, the author and the publisher do not assume and hereby disclaim any liability to any party for any loss, damage, or disruption caused by errors or omissions, whether such errors or omissions result from negligence, accident, or any other cause.

While every effort has been made to avoid any mistake or omission, this publication is being sold on the condition and understanding that neither the author nor the publishers or printers would be liable in any manner to any person by reason of any mistake or omission in this publication or for any action taken or omitted to be taken or advice rendered or accepted on the basis of this work. For any defect in printing or binding the publishers will be liable only to replace the defective copy by another copy of this work then available.

We're really thankful to Almighty Allah for blessing us and for guiding us to follow the right path during our hard times. It gives us great pleasure to thank all those who have made this work possible:
Almighty Allah our families, teachers and our school, who have always supported us and encouraged us to do more than ever and always give our best.
In the end we just want to give a simple message our other mates like other youngsters who are interested in writing and to keep up writing and don't stop don't be ashamed whatever you have written.
We want to tell everyone else to be always happy and believe in Allah, then all your problems will disappear. You should face your problems yourself and try to make the most of your life and don't be bothered by what other people say .

You go ahead just make sure that you won't have any regrets and focus on building yourself.

Contents

Contents

Preface

I'm Diya Farooq, a 12th grade medical student.
I'm a poet, writer, motivational speaker and a social worker with

my best friend Fakhar.

And we've published our book, "When I Was A Little Girl", wich is a compilation of 29 poems, and a few articles and solo poems too.

I've always liked to hang out with my bestie in nature and I also enjoy the time with children, go shopping, play outside and like talking to people and go out to socialize

Acknowledgements

I am Fakhar Injella, a 12th grade medical student.
I'm a poet, writer, motivationaI speaker and a social worker with my best friend Diya
And we've published our book, "When I Was A Little Girl", wich is a compilation of 29 poems, and a few articles and solo poems too.

ACKNOWLEDGEMENTS

I've always loved to read random articles and books about self help I also like sleeping, watching TV working out and making people laugh.
Besides that I've always loved to hang out with my bestie usually in nature cuz we both like it.
That'd be it ig!

Prologue

This book is a collection of 29 poems written by Fakhar Injella and Diya Farooq Shah together . These poems are based on musings of a 13 year old young girl. She keenly observes everything around her. She expresses her perceptions in her own words in a different way, which find an outlet into poetry.

The words used are simple, displaying the beauty of innocent emotions.These poems fill the reader's mind with an image of the life of a little girl and the beauty surrounding her. These poems motivate the readers to live their life to the fullest at the same time taking an inspiration from experience of a little girl. Readers can explore the life in Kashmir through the eyes of a

little girl through these poems. Different parts of her life are mentioned in this book, such as the relationship between a little girl and her family and friends. Her life in different seasons of Kashmir such as autumn and winter and various emotions like depression, regret and nostalgia with reference to her past life as a little girl are represented.

CHAPTER ONE

WHEN I WAS A LITTLE GIRL

Ah!I was so little to understand
That I am good as a little girl
Brightening a wish upon the window
Of my mind, a keen desire...
If! could be a grown up
And while lI'm a grown up
Now, I understand that
Those days of my past...
Were the best days of my life
When I was a little girl
I had nothing to do but 'joy
That was the charm of my life
And moved carefree with the breeze
That stroke my hair as
I ran to catch butterflies
In the park of my house
Those days of my past...
Were the best days of my life
When was a little girl
But time reminds me
Now, I have grown up
Everything I have but,
Nothing in real and no love

No joy, no life with care
There's no peace and happiness too
The stressed thoughts
The depression in the emotions
The tension forbearing my soul
    Kills me and pierces into my heart
if you want me dead
Oh! My life
Go ahead and pick
The gun of stress,
Depression and
Tension
And shoot me!
When I was a little girl
had no money but enough time
And now when
I own money but I have no time...
I lean on my thoughts of future,
Where I won't live life
I know I shall have money
And time too
But shall miss the strength then
I knowI shall get those massive
Lines dug deep by struggle...
So, I want to be a little girl
Again, past in the time
Those were the best days of my life
When I was a little girl

    "You are naughty wher you are small, you are smart when you have grown up. So, don't make your life stressful be naughty act smart."- Diya Farooq & Fakhar injella

CHAPTER TWO

THE BROKEN INN

The old man slept in a broken inn
The inn was haunted he didn't know
Then came the innkeeper
He was a ghost you know
He talked to the old man
The old man said;
"l am an old man
Sleeping in this old inn!"
The ghost fed him with flesh and blood
The old man was scared
He ran for his life...
But the door was closed
The ghost made him sleep forever
"Oh no, I fell from the bed!
Was this a nightmare?
I willnever sleep here
For this is a broken inn,
That lets in, all kinda ghosts."

CHAPTER THREE

MY LIFE IN WINTER

The foggy streets I walked through
And the long coat I wore
I walked in the morning
To reach the school early
And later in the evening
I walked through the market
Again I reached the same street
And watched the dying trees
I reached my home hurriedly
And sat near the fireplace
I thanked god for saving me
From the threatening chill outside
These are my memories...
From the winter in the past

CHAPTER FOUR

MOM

She used to feed us when we were hungry
She used to rock us when we felt sleepy
She used to pat us when we cried
She used to be with us when we were young
She was the one who didn't sleep for nights together
She cared for us, she helped us
She fought for us, she cried for us...
It does matter what we gave her
And it does matter what we did to her
We gave her pain in place of sympathy
We left her alone in place of company
We rendered her miserable, longing for happiness
We broke her heart in place of pampering her
She was the 'One' because of whom
We came into being,
She is our Mother

"See how deep mother's love is! She will walk bore feet, but on your feet she wants to see branded shoes. She will wake long hours to treat your iliness but will specificatly find time to sing us a lullaby" - Diya Faraoq & Fakhar Injella

CHAPTER FIVE

MY CHILDHOOD

When I was a little girl
My dad brought a bicycle for me
I remember that day clearly
It was my most memorable day...
Ah! What a bicycle it was
I rode it happily around
It was red and black in colour I recall
Oh, what a beauty it was!
I went to the lake cycling,
Where I met a girl alone
We were best friends afterwards
We often went to the lake
On my bicycle we went
We rested there quite a while
Oh! The shimmering lake we saw
Watching the beauty of the sky
We turned to our bicycle
It was stolen, OMG!
We both missed it, life had no fun without it
Our bicycle it was
Our passion it was
... I lost the bicycle but got a friend
And she is worth a million
I little care for having lost my bicycle...

"Children are happy because they dont have a file in their minds colled; "All the things that should go wrong' " - Marrainne William Son

SETTING LIFE

When the sun rose,
It's rays fell
Deep in the ocean
Birds woke willingly
Water flowed merrily
But why my life...
Still you are sleeping
In the dark room
Where no moon shines
And no sun rises
Unaware of the outer world
You sleep soundly here
Come out of the room
Or else you will be dead
But wait a minute, what I see.
Alas! It is too late,
My life lies dead
In this dark room
"Darkness connot drive out darkness, only light can do that. Hate can't drive out hate, only love can do that." - Martin Luther King jr

CHAPTER SEVEN

VACATIONS OF PAST WINTER

Apart from school
Tuition is the place where we study
With the feeling of joy
I remember my life in awesome tuitions
Where with the feeling of freedom
We make new friends
We learn new things
It felt like something exotic
We were friendly to teachers too
They supported us and guided us
In every aspect it was unique
Each morning with a happy hope
Forsaying the coming time
While in the break
We talked and talked and played a lot
We went to the canteen
And shared our food
We got time to refresh
We got opportunity to learn something new
We spent time to enjoy our life
And we lived the life of tuitions there
It was the place, where we came to know ourselves.

"Tutions are the best place to regain your curiosity where we learn happily with each other, No force to read or write or to coampete the syllabus." - Diya Farooq & Fakhar Injella

CHAPTER EIGHT

DYING DREAM

Pulled by horses a carriage came
Like a ghust of wind, it came
Like a cloud of smoke, it came
It took my soul
Away went
Away from the world
Alone I was there
In the court of immrotals
My good and bad deeds were weighed
The angels stared at me
I was then pushed through a gate
A house stood in front of me
Were these my good deeds
Or bad ones
Which approached me in the dream
  "While I thought that I was learning to live, I have been learning
how to die." - Leonardo da Vinci

CHAPTER NINE

WE NEED SUPPORT

Freedom we need
To achieve our dreams
To fulfill our desires
To bath in happiness
And to be successtul
We need support from you
And support from the fanily too
And guidance from teachers
And from the society we live in...
Bond and hope from every relation too
The freedom of thoughts
And action shall earn us our dreams
If we are hit or blocked
We shall never ever withstand to start again
If we are prohibited to take steps along
Hope shall never come and
We shall never be permitted again
To be successful, we need support
If you knife our wings
The dreams of desire shall cease to fly
If you imprison our liberty
The thread of life shall break into beads
The depressed youth needs freedom
Or else the hope shall die...

And world shall live no more

CHAPTER TEN

CANDLE AND A MOTH

The candle burns itself
And enlightens the whole world
Moth takes birth
To just enjoy itself
Moth is fond of light
Lost in the search of light it is
The search is endles...
Wandering here and there
Candle stands at one place
Waiting for its end
Helping everyone by its light
Candle burns and moth encircles it
Moth knows its end lies in the candle light
But still it goes on in search of light
It realizes its dream to meet the light...

"We should de anything to help anyone. Anything we can do, we should do." - Diya Farooq & Fakhar Injella

DREAMS

Floating in thc sea of dreams
It's like doing everything
Swimming in the Pacific
Riding on the dinosaurs
From the glasses of dreams
We can see anything
X-ray of snakes
Climbing the Everest
whlle you are in
Your cozy bed at home
You can fly as a bird
And swim like a fish
The future you can see
Past you already know
Meeting the mermaids
Having tea with aliens
It is not everything you see
A cruise in the air
And many more

CHAPTER TWELVE

TEACHERS

Everything in our life acts as a teacher
Our first teacher is our mother
School teachers let us know our life
Friends teach us to enjoy our life
Father teaches us to be responsible
Religion teaches us the way of life
Leaders teach us how to lead
Doctors teach us how to cure
Engineers teach us how to build
And books teach us everything

CHAPTER THIRTEEN

I am not the bird you keep in cages
I am eagle, the king of skies
I am not the eraser which erases mind
I am pen, the writer of thoughts
I am not the anger which discourages you
I am happiness, which teaches you how to live
I am not the darkness of evil
I am light, which enlightens your heart
I am not the book you keep in library
I am thought, which is created in mind
I am not a computer, in which you would just feed data
I am man, the independent inventor
    "You have brains in your head, you have feet in your shoes, you can steer yourself in any direction you choose. You are on your own and you know what you know and you are
the one who decide where to go." - Doctor Seuss

CHAPTER FOURTEEN

THE MILLION DOLLAR SMILE

Millions and millions of dollars
I can spare
The whole world and everyone
I can spare
The past the present and the future
I can spare
For the most expensive thing
I can't let go
Is her million dollar smile
As it is the sparkle of my eye
   "Ever since happiness has heard your name, it has been running through the streets to find you." - Hafez

BETRAYING FRIENDSHIP

Four friends were we
Played together
We read together
We shared together
We talked together
Our friendship went long
Along on the horse of time
Our friendship went by...
Instead of strengthening
The bond became weaker
The days passed, war was afoot
It was not us who split
But she who went away
She betrayed us, condemned us
But we stil thought of her as a friend
She didn't even look at us
But we cared for her
Yet, nobody should be cursed,
Over such betrayal...
Because friendship is a relation
That requires a mighty bond
of forever living moments
And joy of togetherness
But then the tragedy of separation

Hits the hawk at the beak
Friend is the one
Who stays forever
Together by your side
   "Our friend is the best part of our life. So, a friend should not be fake, otherwise our life will be fake." - Diya Farooq & Fakhar lnjella

THE VALLEY OF KASHMIR

Starting an eye over the vast valley
The greenery is spread all over
Winter is on the mountains
And autumn in Char Chinar
Spring we celebrate in Mughal Gardens
Whereas the summer passes in houseboats of Dal Lake
Journey through the Shikaras to those religious shrines
Where we offer Salah in Eid Gah on Eid
The taste of traditional Noon Chai made in Samawars
And the tasty Wazwaan in wedding ceremonies
Qahwa is served with the taste of saffron
Singing the melodies of traditional Kashmir
And dancing the traditional dance Rouf
The beautiful jewellery worn by women
They play Tumakhnaris on wedding ceremonies
The designer Phirans worn by the women
Kangris which are used under the Phirans
And the cold is replaced by warmth underneath
Swimming races in the Jhelum river
The cool Breeze felt while cycling
Along the river side of Kashmir
And the view of Kashmir

Stays blooming with beauty in every eye.

CHAPTER SEVENTEEN

AUTUMN

The yellowing of leaves I see
The cool Breeze I felt on my face
When I ran down to the river
To fetch some water for mother
She would make me some hot chocolate today
Iremember every single creature of that time
When I was a little girl
I remember everything clearly
When the leaves fell from the trees
The migration of birds from here to there
I remember myself looking through the window
Up in the sky patched with clouds
The gathering of leaves by grandpa
To burn them to chase the chill away
I remember myself in the garden
Climbing up the tree to keep a watch from up there
Again I remember myself in the apple orchard
Hanging a hammock tor me
Eating an apple secretly
I walted for winter eagerly
I remember everything clearly
The dying of trees
And yellowing of leaves
The breeze waved cool when

ants busied gathering food for winter
signs sang telling Autumn had come.

SCHOOL LIFE

The first day when
We stepped into school
We cried and cried
And now when we are
leaving this lovely school
Tears swim in our eyes
We cried in the past too
For the love of our family then.
But now, we have realised
Our school is our family
Past in the time, teachers calmed us
And now again our teachers
Who had taught us then, to stay calm
Are bidding goodbye
We met some children
Who became our friends later
But now we don't know
Whether they shall stay with us...
We have a new life ahead
Teachers scolded us for our mistakes
We used to feel forlorn
But now when we see them
Our heart wants to kiss their hands
As those very hands

had at times punished us
But fed us and taught us love as well
   "Youth is the gift of nature but age is a work of art." - Stanllislan
Jerzy Lec

CHAPTER NINETEEN

WISHES

Anytime it could be
Any place it would be
Any festival it may be
Every time we make wishes
We smile, we cry
We laugh and try
We make wishes
We sow desires
We jump, we leap
We skate, break and weep
We make wishes
we sow desires
Be it a birthday
or any other party
Sinking heart on result day
Strained brow in calamity
We make wishes
We sow desires
To fulfill our dreams
We make wishes
To accomplish our wishes
We sow desires

CHAPTER TWENTY

READING AN AVENTURE

Reading leads to adventure
I may go anywhere
Sights see me smiling in the sky
I am the one with Mr Columbus...
Anywhere I can go exploring the world
The excitement around in the faces
Of creatures hails me...
While I am still, sitting in my study
Enclosed within the comfortable chair of mine
In the calmness and peace of my room
But the journey through the books
Is but a road of endeavour
That leads me to adventures
The winged chariot of mind
Takes me away
To meet the fairies in unknown lands
Or else have tea with the whale.

CHAPTER TWENTY-ONE

HUMANITY

No separate religion should lie here
No rivalry should dwell in between
We all are humans
And we all live on the same planet
So, why should we fight?
We all are close
We should support each other
We all have one creator
But the only difference that rules
We may call Him with different names
Yet no religion teaches us
To kill our brothers
So, we all should accept,
The supreme religion of humanity
"To be a good human, try to help every human." - Diya Farooq &
Fakhar Injella

CHAPTER TWENTY-TWO

SPRING

Every time l look up in the sky
Colourful kites I find everywhere
Smooth and cool is the breeze that
Touches me while playing in the garden
Little buds, ready to bloom
Cherry blossoms so beautiful I find
Animals waken stark, to live life again
Green grass that carries dew drops
Freshens up my morning
Air that I breathe...
The little cold in the evening
Makes me wear a sweater sleeved
Children going to school
Returning merry and wiser back home
Happiness I mark in their eyes
Winter's harsh days are gone
Now, I can see the joy of spring
That breathes in life in everything

"Spring will come und so will happiness, hold on ife will get warmer." - Anita Krizzar

CHAPTER TWENTY-THREE

TIME NEVER WAITS

Away it goes
It does not wait
Not for the old man
Walking on the road
Not even for the child
Running down the street
It does not wait
Not for the lady
Waiting at the stop
Not even for the vendor
Waiting for customers
It does not wait
Neither for the driver
Nor for the passengers
Not even for the waiting man
Who is waiting for someone
It does not wait
And we also should not wait
For time to wait on us
As it does not wait
And away it goes.

CHAPTER TWENTY-FOUR

IF I HAD A BROTHER

If I had a brother
I would have played with him
I would have enjoyed with him
Only, if I had a brother
We would have lived life together
We would have gone for shopping together
Only, if I had a brother
He would have been my protector
He would have been my jester
Only, if I had a brother
I would never leave him alone
I would accompany him everywhere
Only, if I had a brother
He would have been my big brother
And I would have been his little sister
Only, if I had a brother

"You learn more about life from watching 'Big Brother' than from reading a book." - John de Mol jr

CHAPTER TWENTY-FIVE

LONELY STREET

It stood alone,
All night and day
Lone street I called it
I did walk alone there
When I saw a shadow
It was dark and tall
I was frightened
Nobody came to help
Everybody just watched
Everyone just laughed at me
Nobody cared for me
At that lone hour
So, I called it the lone street
Because nobody came to help
While I suffered alone
As it was the lone street
That stood alone

"I have accepted fear as part of life specifically the fear of change... I have gone ahead despite the pounding in the heart that says 'Turn back!' " - Erica Jong

CHAPTER TWENTY-SIX

WINNERS

People who win to defeat others
Are but losers and not winners
And those who lose to win others
Win love of everyone
Hope arises in every heart
Losers are the death of hope
But winners are those,
Who give birth to hope
People who criticize others
Are losers, not winners
But people who let go.
Are real winners
Losers quit when they fail
Winners fail until they succeed
    "Winners don't do different things but may do things differently.
" - Unknown

CHAPTER TWENTY-SEVEN

STRUGGLE

Struggle lies in every heart
In every heart lives a tiny hope
A bird struggles to live it's life
It's struggle lies to find its food
Many days if spent foodless
it struggles to keep alive
The hope then becomes food of life
The period of struggle when comes to man
And harshness of time is tried over him
He surrenders to defeat
And converges hopeless
He takes to death and kills the hope
Why oh man, you are so weak?
Even when god has bestowed on you
Joy of life and the brain of reason
Yet, when god fulfills your desires
Your greed stands as huge as a mountain
You don't even think of the dying
Hungry and poor then
Who are also a creation of god
Don't display your mountain of greed,
And hide It behind the tree of struggle
And when God tests you
Just stand up and get ready to face it

"Champions keeps plaving until they get it right."- Billie Jean King

CHAPTER TWENTY-EIGHT

SAVE DEAR MY MOTHER EARTH

Vast is the space
Never ending it is
One little planet
Our earth it is
So beautiful it was
God's gift it was
The natural beauty,
And the fresh air
Where it went?
Disappearing it is
Crying it is, only for help
So, we should help
We all will help
Together we will,
Save this planet
Together we are
To help this planet
Not I, but we all
Can do this
We all will save
We all will protect
Our dear mother earth

CHAPTER TWENTY-NINE

SAVE TREES SAVE LIFE

They are important in our life
They are the reason of our life
We use them when we need them
We kill them when they need us
We hack and chop and cut them to death
We can see their corpses almost everywhere
In chairs, tables, houses and the wood
Wherein we burn their lives
We should use them
when we need them
But reuse and regrow them as well
After killing the one upstanding tree
Plant in place again the little plant
If you don't plant, no tree shall remain
No animal, no human, and no life shall sustain
So, for the sake of life on the earth
Kill trees less and plant them more

"If trees could scream, we would be so cavaler about cutting them down." - Jack Handey

CHAPTER THIRTY

NOTE BY THE POETS

Note By The Poets:

Something about ourselves:

One day, me and my bestie were feeling bored in the classroom lecture. And just then we hit on an idea

to write a poem. And later on, our interest in writing poems increased. We have been writing poems

since then. As we wrote poems, our friendship also grew stronger, hard enough to break.

About the book:

This book is a collection of 29 poems written by Fakhar Injella and Diya Farooq Shah together. These

poems are based on musings of a 13 year old young girl. She keenly observes everything around her.

She expresses her perceptions in her own words in a different way, which find an outlet into poetry. The

words used are simple, displaying the beauty of innocent emotions.

www.ingramcontent.com/pod-product-compliance
Lightning Source LLC
Chambersburg PA
CBHW021144130726
47988CB00003B/1463